Bright DOG
Bonnie

Books About Bonnie:

Big Dog Bonnie • Best Dog Bonnie

Bad Dog Bonnie • Brave Dog Bonnie

Busy Dog Bonnie • Bright Dog Bonnie

Bright Dog Bonnie

BEL MOONEY

Illustrated by Sarah McMenemy

WALKER
BOOKS

This is a work of fiction. Names, characters, places and
incidents are either the product of the author's imagination
or, if real, used fictitiously.

First published 2010 by Walker Books Ltd
87 Vauxhall Walk, London SE11 5HJ

This edition published 2013

2 4 6 8 10 9 7 5 3 1

Text © 2010 Bel Mooney
Illustrations © 2010 Sarah McMenemy

Photographs pages 86-89 © Robin Allison-Smith

The right of Bel Mooney and Sarah McMenemy to be identified as
author and illustrator respectively of this work has been asserted by
them in accordance with the Copyright, Designs and Patents Act 1988

This book has been typeset in StempelSchneidler

Printed and bound in Great Britain by Clays Ltd, St Ives plc.

British Library Cataloguing in Publication Data:
a catalogue record for this book is available from the British Library

ISBN 978-1-4063-5118-7

www.walker.co.uk

To Elodie and Willow Charles
B.M.

To my wonderful daughter, Georgia
S.M.

✤Naughty Dog✤

Harry had never known Bonnie to be in
such a naughty mood. Not even before
she went for her training because she'd
scratched the postman and stolen a shoe.
Harry smiled when he thought of that
– and maybe that was the problem. As he
said to Susie, the friend he'd met at the
dog training school, "You can't make a dog
good if you think it's funny when she's
naughty."

But one day something happened which didn't make Harry smile. Not one bit. For Bonnie's naughtiness led to something – or rather, some*body* – totally unexpected coming into their lives, and Harry wasn't at all sure it was a good thing.

It had been raining that Saturday morning and Mum was already grumpy. Things got worse when Bonnie jumped out through the cat flap, pottered about  in the garden investigating those funny creatures who lived under the soil, and came back in with muddy paws and a face to match. Which she proceeded to wipe along the side of the

pretty cream-coloured armchair
that Zack and Zena's mum had just given
them because she had no room for it any
more.

"*Aargh!* Bonnie, you naughty dog!"
shouted Mum. "Get your grubby little face
away from my new chair!"

Oops, thought Harry, now it'll be my
fault.

"For goodness' sake, Harry, couldn't you
have stopped her?"

There you go!

He was just about
to protest, when
the telephone rang.
Dad often called
on a Saturday, so
Harry raced over.
The phone was on
the kitchen wall
and he wanted
to reach it before
Mum; he hated the
way her voice went
all funny when she
spoke to Dad.

But she was too quick.
Harry stood by as she said, "Hello? Oh,
Dave?" as if she hardly knew the person on
the other end of the line. He waited as she
complained about the washing machine,
the weather and the dog; and he wondered
why grown-ups didn't realize that the more

they moaned, the worse things seemed.

At last she handed him the phone but waited beside him, which made him feel awkward. All Dad wanted was to ask how school was going and how Harry had done in his last test.

Harry grunted.

"What's with the one-word answers, big guy?" asked Dad.

Harry wondered why grown-ups didn't realize that if they asked you interesting questions, they'd get interesting answers.

"What are you getting me for my birthday, Dad?"

"It's over two months off, Haz! You can email me some requests the week before."

"Oh," said Harry. That was certainly *not* an interesting answer.

He put the phone down and looked up at Mum. When he saw her frowning, he knew he had to get out of there pretty quickly.

"I think I'll take Bonnie next door," he said brightly.

"She needs a walk around the block first."

But when they went back into the living room, the little dog was curled up in a ball on the cream armchair, fast asleep. As well as the muddy smears along the side, there was a pattern of brown paw prints all over the cushion – and suddenly the chair Mum loved didn't look nearly as smart as it had.

Harry was about to joke that now it fitted in better with the rest of their flat, but he saw his mother's face and changed his mind.

"Harry, will you get that animal out of here – NOW!"

He didn't need telling twice.

But in his hurry to escape Harry forgot something very important. Bonnie always wore a collar, but usually they added a harness when they took her for a walk. She had never learned to walk to heel like the show dogs on TV, and the harness stopped her pulling on her neck. Today Harry just clipped the lead to her collar and was out through the front door before Mum could think of getting him to clean up Bonnie's muddy trail.

Luckily the rain had stopped. Mr Wilson was standing outside his house, and he told Harry that Zack and Zena had gone to the supermarket with their mum. Boring! thought Harry. Now he'd have to take Bonnie for a walk as Mum had ordered.

But Bonnie didn't want to go for a walk. She dug her paws in stubbornly, thinking that the soft, warm chair was a much better choice than the cold, damp pavement.

"Come on, Bons!" pleaded Harry.

"Grrrrr!" Bonnie replied, putting her head down like a little white bull.

"Come ON!"

Harry was as fed up with his dog as his mum was. As fed up as his dad was when Mum answered the phone with that cold, distant voice. As fed up as Bonnie was with being pulled around and shouted at. He turned and stomped along the pavement, letting the lead run out to its longest extent, then tugging hard. He *would* make that stubborn little dog obey!

Then suddenly there was nothing on the end of the lead. Nothing … except air and the sparkly black jewelled collar Mum had bought one day in a dressing-up-Bonnie mood. The collar had been fastened too loosely and Bonnie's head had simply slipped through.

After that everything happened very
quickly. Bonnie felt freedom lift her spirits,
and she rushed off the way they had
come, as if this was a
wonderful game. Harry
yelled her name and
started to follow. He
didn't notice a low
grumble coming
nearer and
nearer,
building
to a roar as
a big black
motorcycle tore
round the corner.

Just as Bonnie
decided to run across
the road.

Harry saw the white ball of fluff facing the big black motorbike, heard the engine noise change at the same time as he heard his own voice – almost as if it didn't belong to him – shriek, "BONNIEEEEEEEEE!"

Then it was over. The motorcyclist swerved, wobbled horribly, but managed to stay upright – and stop. Bonnie sat shivering in the middle of the road. Harry rushed forward and scooped her up, imagining in those horrible seconds what it would have been like had she been hit.

He buried his face in her fur and whispered, "You're all right, Little Bear." Somebody was shouting. The motorcyclist was striding towards them. All dressed in leather, his face completely hidden by the helmet, the biker looked like a scary creature from *Doctor Who*.

"What do you think you're doing?"

The helmet came off with a furious yank – and the face frowning at them was just as frightening. The man had a bushy beard and thick, dark hair and his mouth looked very red as it shouted, "I could have been killed!"

"S-s-s-so could my dog," stammered Harry.

"Never mind the stupid little mutt! You ought to be ashamed of yourself, letting a dog run out of control like that."

"S-s-s-she's *not* out of control!" Harry protested, but not very convincingly.

"Yes, she is!" shouted the man.

"No, she's not!" Harry shouted back.

"Yip yip yip yip YIP!" barked Bonnie, who was now over her shock and knew she had to protect Harry from this fierce-looking stranger.

"Shouldn't have a dog if you can't control it!" bellowed the man.

18

"Shouldn't ride a fast bike if you can't control *that*!" yelled Harry.

"Yip, yip, yip!"

You could hear the racket a mile away. No wonder Mum came out, drying her hands on a tea towel and looking worried.

"What's going on?" she asked.

"That dog nearly had me off my bike!"

"He nearly ran Bonnie over," wailed Harry, close to tears now.

The man saw his face. "Well, it didn't happen, did it?" he said gruffly. "No need to get upset."

"I'm NOT upset!" shouted Harry, and Bonnie continued with such a terrible yipping and yapping that the biker and Mum put their hands over their ears.

The man told Mum what had happened, and Harry just listened, head down, because everything he said was true. It *was* all his fault. He waited for his mum to shout at him.

But nothing happened. When he looked up, she was smiling at the man. "Well, you're obviously a very good rider, to control your bike like that," she said.

The man shuffled his feet. "Well, I've been riding for years, you know," he replied with a big grin. "The name's Eddie, by the way."

"Oh, yes … er … I'm Ann," said Harry's mum, sounding flustered.

There was a short silence. Bonnie was

wriggling like mad in Harry's arms, so his mum suggested he take her inside. "Give her a biscuit to calm her down."

"Probably could use one yourself too, eh, lad?" smiled Eddie.

Harry glared at him and turned away.

Back in the house, he snuggled up on the sofa with Bonnie, expecting to hear Mum come in to tell him off at any moment. This was turning out to be a horrible day. He looked at the muddy chair and waited for the storm to break.

It must have been a good twenty minutes later when he heard footsteps, and the front door closing. And laughter. Mum burst into the room – face pink, eyes bright. The biker followed, his helmet under his arm. He seemed to fill the room.

"You'll never guess, love!" she said. "Eddie and I went to the same college!"

Eddie grinned."Yeah, but I was a bit before you."

"Isn't that an amazing coincidence? So I've asked him in for a cup of tea and a piece of cake. It's the least we can do, since Bonnie could have killed him!"

Eddie threw back his head and laughed loudly as if she'd made the funniest joke in the world.

Where was the shouting monster in black? Come to think of it, where was the shouting small dog in white?

Harry couldn't understand it. Bonnie was lying next to him like a little lion, her head held up straight, her coal-black eyes fixed on the stranger. Normally she would be on the floor, yelping like mad. Why, she even still

barked at Mr Wilson, and they'd known him
for ages.

But when this visitor sat down in the
muddy armchair and waited for Harry's
mum to bring in the tea, Bonnie padded over
to sniff at his big biker boots. Eddie said,
"Shall we be friends now, little dog?" and –
to Harry's amazement – Bonnie
licked his
outstretched
finger.

"Your dog likes me, Ann," said Eddie when Mum came in with the tray.

"Not such a silly little dog then, eh?" smiled Mum.

"No way!" said Harry, but nobody seemed interested in his opinion.

"In fact," Eddie said with a wink, "she just might be the brightest dog I've ever met!"

BONNIE was still recovering from
the shock of that big black motorbike roaring
along the road towards her. And as for
the angry monster riding it...

But it was all over now. Here he was in their
home, and somehow everything was all right.
The man smelled of leather and leaves and lots
of interesting things, and Bonnie knew
there was something good about him.
Dogs can always tell. Usually she
didn't want anybody (except those children
next door, and the girl with the
annoying chihuahua) to come onto
the territory that belonged to her pack.
But this man was different.

Bonnie could sniff the difference in the air.
It was making Mum laugh out loud — and that
is the most beautiful sound to a dog.

❖Dancing Dog❖

Harry, Zack, Zena and Susie all went to the same school now. Most of the time it was fun, but these days Harry wasn't so sure. It was all because of the Great Dance Craze. It made him feel just as out of sorts as the fact that Eddie kept coming round to see Mum.

He wanted things to go back to the way they were.

The problem of the GDC began (of course) with *Strictly Come Dancing* on television. Zena and her parents were addicted, and even Zack secretly liked the show – although he pretended he just watched it to keep them all company. Harry used to think Zena was cool because she wasn't really a *girly* girl, but now she kept waltzing around the room or jumping about doing the salsa and talking about what colour sparkly dress she'd wear to do a cha-cha – and it was all getting ridiculous.

When Susie came round it was worse, since the two girls got even more excitable together, wriggling and shimmying and rocking and rolling, while Bonnie and Princess Daisy the (annoying) chihuahua hopped about at their feet, almost in time to the music.

As for Zack, he was actually quite a good dancer, which didn't help Harry one bit. Zack would flex his biceps like an old-fashioned muscleman and point out that male professional dancers were just as strong as boxers, but *much* better looking.

"That rules you out, then," snorted his sister.

"Let's show you how to dance, Harry!" called Susie, holding out a hand.

"You've got to be joking," he said, backing away in a hurry.

At that Zena swept Bonnie up in her arms, held one of her paws out straight in a dancers' hold, and twirled round and round the room until the poor little dog looked dizzy.

"Give me my dog back!" Harry demanded. "She doesn't like dancing."

"Course she does," said Susie. "All girls like dancing. Don't we, Daisy?"

The (annoying) chihuahua yapped in agreement.

Harry watched in despair as his friends replayed the last episode so that the girls could study the dance moves. Even Zack looked fascinated. Harry slumped on his cushion, longing for the old days when they would all just muck about in the garden with Bonnie. As always, his pet sensed he was feeling down and snuggled up to him.

It was Zena who had the awful idea. Suddenly she clapped her hands and said, "I know! Let's start a dance club at school! Everybody'll be up for it!"

"We could have a competition," said her twin.

"You'd be bound to win, Zack," smiled Susie.

"Only if *you* dance with me," he replied, with a gallant bow.

Ugh! That's it, thought Harry – the world really *has* gone mad. He sat in silence while the others bubbled over with plans for their contest.

"I bet Mrs Barnes will teach us. She loves *Strictly* and she nearly went professional when she was young."

"We should just do one dance – the salsa!" said Susie.

"Oh, but I love the waltz – it's *soooo* romantic," sighed Zena, waving her arms like butterfly wings.

"OK, maybe two dances," said Zack, "one Latin and one ballroom."

They chattered away, and nobody noticed Harry's silence. Except Bonnie. She looked at him with worried eyes, and tried to get his attention by chasing Princess Daisy round and round the cushion he sat on.

It didn't work.

But Zena tripped over the two little dogs as she did another spin to show the others how it was done – and tumbled in a heap, hitting Harry with her elbow.

"Ow!" he yelled.

"Are you OK?" asked Susie.

"Sorry, Harry!" said Zena.

Having the girls fuss over him made Harry feel a bit better, but it didn't last long.

"So we're all agreed then? We'll all go and see Mrs Barnes together?" demanded Zack.

The girls cried "Yay!" in chorus, but Harry said nothing.

"Haz?"

Harry shrugged. "Dunno."

"What d'you mean, *dunno*? Aren't you in with us?" asked Zena.

Susie frowned. "We *have* to be a team, Harry."

"You're not being chicken, are you?" asked Zack with a grin.

"NO!"

"Then what?" Zena asked, folding her arms.

There was a silence. In those seconds so many thoughts to explain his mood flitted through Harry's head. He wanted to tell them that he didn't like his mum having a boyfriend;

35

it was all wrong. He didn't like the fact that his dad hardly ever phoned now – and never got round to suggesting visits. He didn't like Dad being sarcastic when Harry let it slip that Eddie rode a motorbike. And he didn't like *dancing*.

Although a small voice inside told him that this wasn't strictly true. He didn't know about dancing. He was afraid of being useless at dancing.

He was *embarrassed*.

"I … er … I just don't fancy it," he mumbled.

To his horror, Zena looked so downcast he thought she might burst into tears.

"But, Haz, who'll be my partner if you don't join in?"

"Zack, of course."

"No way am I dancing with my sister! Me and Susie are gonna steal the show." Harry felt five pairs of eyes fixed on him,

waiting for his reply. Bonnie and Princess
Daisy were sitting at Zena's feet, as if
they understood every single word
that had been said and were
encouraging him to join in.

"Har–reee?" pleaded Zena.

"Sorry, guys," he
muttered, and bolted for
the door. He had to get out
of there as fast as he could,
before they could see his

expression. He
didn't even
bother to make
sure Bonnie was following him.

He was relieved to see there was no big
black motorbike outside their flat. He just
wanted to escape to his room and cuddle
Bonnie in peace without having to tell Mum
what was wrong.

No chance.

When he pushed open the door to the living room he saw Eddie sitting cradling a mug of tea in his hands as usual – and then from nowhere it was as if a whirlwind had hit Bonnie and him, knocking them both sideways. This was a whirling, twirling, jumping, bounding, sliding, bounding, jumping creature. This was an ink blot come to life. A miniature black sheep gone mad. A tiny dark cloud come to earth to create a storm wherever it went.

It was a very small black poodle.

Bonnie squared up to this intruder

on her territory before you could say, "Brave dog!" She set up such a furious yapping that Eddie covered his ears with his hands. "Here, boy! Here, Bruce!" he called.

When some calm had been restored –
which is to say, when the small black poodle
was struggling in Eddie's arms and Bonnie
was wriggling just as angrily in Harry's –
Harry asked, *"Bruce?"*

"That's right. He's my sister's dog. She
made me agree to mind the mutt while
she's at this wedding. Tried to get out of it,
but you know what women are like." He
winked, and Harry's mum gave that silly
little giggle Harry heard so
much these days.

Harry stared at the poodle, who glared at Bonnie with a *"Grrrrr."*

"Very scary!" said Harry. Then he started to laugh. For the first time that day great gusts of laughter shook him, and he had to put Bonnie down before he dropped her.

"Yeah, I know," grinned Eddie. "That's what I think too. Bit of a joke dog if you ask me. But you'll like my sister, Ann."

He smiled at Harry's mum with that soppy look Harry had noticed all too often, and she simpered back, all pink and pretty. Harry knew he should be pleased, but it was so embarrassing to watch his mother behaving like a *kid*.

Eddie put Bruce
down and the two
dogs raced around
the room, barking
at each other but
with tails wagging
like mad. Then they
faced one another and
darted from side to side.

"They look like
they're dancing!"
laughed Mum.
"Oh no!"
groaned Harry,
remembering
his problem.

He sat down and
told them all about the
plan for a dance club, and how he felt he
was letting his friends down but couldn't
bear the thought of it.

"Why?" Eddie asked.

"I *hate* dancing!" Harry snapped.

"But you've never even had a go!" his mum protested.

"The thing is, Harry, mate – you've got to make a choice."

Harry scowled at Eddie. "What d'you mean?"

"You've got to choose between two fears."

"I'm NOT scared of anything!" Harry said loudly, but Eddie went on as if he hadn't spoken.

"You've got to decide which is worse, see: looking a bit daft or upsetting your friends."

Harry wasn't convinced.

"Tell you what, I'll show you," said Eddie.

"What?"

"How to dance, of course!"

"Don't tell me you can dance as well?" trilled Harry's mum. "You're *so* full of surprises, Ed!"

"Yeah, well. Our little secret, mind," he mumbled. "So what d'you say, Harry?"

"Yip yip," said Bonnie, doing a tiny twirl.

Ten minutes later Mrs Wilson found three visitors on their doorstep. Susie had gone but Zack and Zena jumped up in surprise when Bonnie tore into the sitting room, closely followed by Bruce. The two dogs danced around in circles.

"What's *that*?" Zena cried.

"That's Bruce the miniature poodle," Harry told her. "And before you ask, yes, he probably *is* named after Bruce Forsyth."

When they'd finished laughing at the two dancing dogs, they all fell silent. Harry knew his friends were waiting for him to say something.

"The thing is," he began, "I don't really *like* dancing, but I'll give it a go for you guys. Just as long as you don't tread on my toes, Zena. Or make me wear sequins."

"Promise I won't, Harry. I'll wear enough sequins for both of us! Oh, I'm so excited!"

"No taking sneaky lessons, mind," said Zack. "I still want to win."

"As if!" joked Harry.

But he could have sworn Bonnie and Bruce both looked up and smiled.

**BONNIE wondered why Harry
was in such a bad mood all the time,
glaring at that big man his mum liked so much
and who made her so cheerful. Then Harry**

was cross with his friends too. She could
smell his unhappiness on her own fur
as he cuddled her.

But now it all felt different — and it
was all thanks to that funny black poodle.
Of course Bruce was a bit stupid and noisy,
and almost as annoying as Princess Daisy,
but he came to see them and suddenly
everybody was cheerful again.

That's what I call a result, Bonnie thought sleepily
as she snuggled down on Harry's bed. And Bruce
was sort of cute, for a daft poodle.

Surprise Dog

Harry decided that life was as full of surprises as the best kind of Christmas Day. Who would have thought that the tiny white dog his mum had got from the RSPCA home would have turned out to be so *big* and brave? Not to mention being so bright that she always seemed to know how to solve problems.

And who would have thought that Mum's new friend – the scary bearded biker who'd ridden into their lives on a big black motorcycle – would be so light on his feet?

"This is how you hold your arms, Haz," Eddie instructed, pulling Harry's mum up for a waltz, and whirling her around until her ponytail fell down and she couldn't stop laughing.

"Your turn now, Haz. I'll be the girl!"

These days their flat was always full of music: the waltz, the cha-cha, the quickstep, the rumba, the salsa. Harry was training Bonnie to dance on her back legs whenever he held up a chicken treat, and she could keep time with the music just as well as he could.

But today she flopped down and looked at him as if to say, "*You* dance!"

"You've been overfeeding her, Harry," said Mum, picking her up and stroking her silky ears.

"Yes, she's getting a bit chubby," smiled Eddie. "Mind you, us blokes like something to cuddle!" And he tickled Mum until she squeaked.

Yuck, thought Harry. "Er … shall we get on with the lesson?"

An hour later he reckoned he could do a pretty good waltz, and when he practised with Mum she agreed.

"Shh – no telling Zack and Zena," he said. "I want everybody to think I'm a natural."

Zack was disappointed that the school had decided against a dance competition, even though Mrs Barnes had been brilliant at helping them organize the dance club. "Me and Susie would've scored a row of tens!" he boasted, while his sister rolled her eyes.

"It's better this way," Zena said. "If we just do a demonstration on parents' evening, nobody will have their feelings hurt if they're rubbish."

"Talking of rubbish – how come you told us you couldn't dance?" asked Zack, giving Harry a little smack on his arm.

"Yes, partner, you're quite a star!" said Zena, sounding really surprised.

"S'pose it must be in my blood," said Harry modestly.

"We'll be able to dance at your birthday party, Harry!" called Susie, who had just arrived with Princess Daisy, who was pulling on her lead.

As usual, the Maltese and the chihuahua immediately started their ear-splitting chorus of yelps and yaps, then chased each other about until they were tired. Harry was surprised to see Bonnie give in first. But the girls hadn't forgotten the subject he wanted to avoid. Not dancing this time, but his birthday party.

"Is your dad coming?" asked Zena.

Harry shrugged. "Hasn't made his mind up yet."

That night, safe and warm in bed, Bonnie snuggled up beside him, Harry confided in his pet. Mr and Mrs Wilson had offered to hold the birthday party at their house, because they had more room there than in Harry's flat. Everybody was looking forward to it, but Harry hadn't told anyone the big snag.

He didn't want a party unless his dad promised to be there, but his dad didn't want to come and meet Eddie. Harry didn't expect him to come to parents' evening, because he never had, but his birthday party *mattered*.

"It's so *stupid*, Bons," Harry whispered in the dark. "I mean, he's happy living with Kim; and now that Mum's happy cos Eddie's around, she says she doesn't mind meeting Kim at last; but Dad's just being childish. And I'm stuck in the middle. What am I supposed to do? Why do grown-ups have to spoil things?"

Bonnie closed her eyes and made a soft sound almost like a mew. How was she to know?

"Makes me really miserable, Mouse-Face," sighed Harry.

Bonnie opened her eyes and stared at him. *That* much she certainly knew.

There were only twenty-four children in the dance club, and Mrs Barnes was telling them what was going to happen on parents' evening. She smiled. "You're the entertainment, so after the mums and dads have heard how their little darlings could work harder and talk less in class, they'll all be given a glass of wine and asked to sit down to watch you lot – *strictly* to cheer them up, you see?"

Most of the children laughed, but Harry whispered to Zena, "Sounds strictly scary."

"You'll be fine. You're brilliant!" she whispered back.

"Now, who's going to do which dance?" asked Mrs Barnes. "First, the waltz…"

"No," Harry whispered. "Let's go for the salsa."

But the voice inside him was muttering, Get me out of here! It didn't help that Zack and Susie seemed to be volunteering for every single dance, while suddenly he was wishing he'd never agreed to take part. It was all Eddie's fault.

No, it wasn't. It was Dad's fault for not agreeing to come to his birthday party.

The truth was, everything was getting mixed up in his head. How on earth was he going to be able to remember the dance steps?

A week later it was the Big Night. The girls had been told to wear pretty dresses, which was easy for them. But the boys had been told to look smart, which certainly *wasn't* easy. Mum had bought Harry some new jeans, and now she held out one of her blouses to show him. It was bright orange, with frills down the front.

"Look, this is perfect for salsa," she beamed.

"What?" gasped Harry. "A girl's blouse? An *orange* girl's blouse?"

Fortunately Eddie saved the day by handing him a parcel. In it was a blue shirt patterned all over with palm trees and fruit. "It's mine, all the way from Cuba, home of the salsa," he explained. "It's got genuine Latin spirit and my sis cut it down to fit you."

"Oh, love, you're so thoughtful," said Harry's mum.

It was true. Eddie *was* thoughtful – and the shirt was kind of cool.

But the snag came when Eddie said he couldn't stay in the flat to look after Bonnie as he'd promised. He had to meet a friend to talk business.

"Sorry, Ann, but you can take the pooch along, can't you?"

"Mmm, well, it's too long to leave her – especially as she's been a bit off colour lately. No one will notice her in my bag."

Harry groaned. Some of the boys at school still laughed at Bonnie because she was so small, and tonight he didn't want *any* distractions…

The dance club waited behind the stage. Some (like Zack) looked confident and couldn't wait to start the demonstration. Others (like Harry) quaked at the thought of performing in public. Still, Harry thought Zena looked lovely in her blue dress with ruffles and sparkly silver shoes.

"It's the same colour as your shirt." She smiled shyly. "We're a perfect match!"

Harry tried to smile back but the smile sort of got stuck. It was as if he were a robot who hadn't been programmed properly. His arms and legs felt as stiff as his face; and he knew that if he spoke, it would come out as a scratchy croak, like a hinge that needed oil. What were his teachers saying to Mum about his schoolwork? He knew he hadn't been concentrating lately, what with the dancing and the worrying over Dad. And Mum. And Eddie. And Kim. It wasn't fair. How could you make room in your brain for school stuff when all the other worries were crowding it out?

Zack's voice seemed to be coming from miles away. "Earth to Hazza… Earth to Hazza."

"Hello!" said Susie. "Wakey-wakey!"

"We have to go to the side of the stage. It's nearly time," said Zena.

Harry glanced around. His friends were all looking at him, puzzled. Some of the other children were also staring. He couldn't bear it.

But he had to *try* – for Zena's sake.

There was an excited buzz in the hall as Mrs Barnes walked onto the stage and explained about the dance club. "The children have been working hard on their dances and we hope that next term even more will join the group. This isn't a competition; we just want to show you all that exercise can be as much fun as this!"

Then somebody put on the first track, and four couples went out onto the stage to waltz round and round, smiling all the time as they had been taught.

"Look how brilliant Zack and Susie are," whispered Zena, but Harry couldn't see a thing. There was a mist in front of his eyes, his heart was thumping and his knees were weak. He'd never been so frightened in his life.

Then Zena whispered, "Come on, Harry – it's our turn!"

He heard the first few bars of the familiar music – a track they'd practised to a hundred times. He started to walk out, holding Zena's hand high in the air … but then he stopped.

Froze.

Seized up.

It was as if they were playing statues – except the music hadn't stopped.

Harry could see Zena looking desperate as she walked all around him with high steps, like a real dancer, trying to pretend that this was part of their routine. The other dancers were crowding at the side of the stage, staring at him. It was terrible. A man in the audience laughed.

It was then that the miracle happened. A small white ball of fluff tore down the aisle, raced up the steps and flew across the stage. The happy rhythms of the salsa filled the air as Bonnie started to dance. She raised herself on her hind legs like Harry had taught her and jumped in time to the music, waving her front paws in the air. Zena danced around her – and somehow Harry forgot all about his stage fright. Bonnie had come to rescue him.

The three of them danced a salsa like nobody had ever seen, and all the parents laughed and clapped and cheered. Then, couple by couple, the other dancers joined them on stage. But as they swayed and

twirled around her, Bonnie lay down in the
middle and gave a short, strange bark.

The music stopped and Harry saw his
mum coming towards the stage with a huge
smile on her face. He saw Mr and Mrs Wilson
too … but who was this? A man with glasses
was pushing past Mum, not taking his eyes
off Bonnie, who lay still and panting.

"Is this your dog?" he asked Harry.

"Sure is!" Harry said proudly.

"We'd better get her home right away. I'm a vet, and I'm fairly certain that she's whelping."

"What does that mean?" asked Mum.

"Puppies!" said the vet. "This little lady's about to have puppies!"

BONNIE wasn't afraid. She was warm and safe in the cardboard box, with a couple of old towels and some newspapers beneath her.
The man with the glasses had gentle hands and was helping her do this important work, while Mum was stroking her head.

Where was Harry? She heard his worried voice in the distance – "How is she?" – and the man said, "Nearly there now."

Oh, but what a special feeling this was! Suddenly there was a tiny squirming creature in front of her and she knew she had to lick, lick, lick to welcome it into the world.

Then another ... *lick, lick, lick.*

"She hasn't finished," whispered the man. And Bonnie stopped licking to concentrate on one last push for one last pup.

Another tiny squirmer!

And then Harry was there, saying, "What a clever girl, what a clever girl!" over and over again.

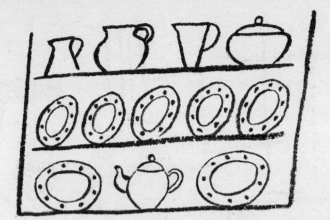

Bright Dog

Yes, thought Harry, you *never* knew what was going to happen next.

"Bonnie's given me the best birthday present ever," he said as he stared down into the big cardboard box where his dog lay with the sweetest, smallest puppies in the whole world.

"Who'd have thought she was pregnant!" marvelled his mum.

"You told me I'd been feeding her too much!" said Harry.

"And yet she ran up onto that stage to help you dance," said Mum, shaking her head in amazement.

"No wonder the puppies started to come," said Eddie.

The three of them couldn't stop gazing at the tiny white mummy-dog and her minuscule brood, cosy in the warmest corner of the kitchen.

"Have you given Bruce the news yet?" asked Harry.

"Yes, and he's in a state of shock," said Eddie. "He's got to save up to buy them all collars and leads!"

They all laughed.

Between them Bonnie and Bruce had produced a litter which looked like both of them. One puppy was completely white, but the other two had splodges of black on their white coats, and one of them had two black ears.

The puppies looked like little blind mice at first – they were only about twelve centimetres long – but they were getting bigger every day. Bonnie was a good mother: she fed them and licked them clean and snuggled down with them as if she'd been practising for this all her life. Harry's mum was reading all about how to look after Bonnie and her puppies in her book on Maltese dogs.

"They'll open their eyes in about ten days," Mum told Harry.

"Just in time for your birthday party!" said Eddie.

"But they won't be able to walk until after that," Mum warned, "so everybody will have to be really gentle with them."

"We'll make it like hospital hours," said Harry seriously, "and just let people visit for a short while."

When the twins popped round to see the puppies, Zena could hardly speak; all that came out of her mouth was *"Aaaah!"*

"Wow," said Zack. "Did you know Super-Wabbit had a boyfriend, Haz?"

"Course not!"

"So what d'you call puppies like this?" asked Zena.

"Mum says they're maltipoos. Half Maltese, half miniature poodle."

Zack snorted, then clapped a hand over his mouth in case he frightened the puppies. "*Poos?* You can't call puppies *poos!*"

"Whatever they are," sighed Zena, "they're gorgeous."

"Have you told your father yet?" asked Mum casually.

Harry hadn't. Each time he went to pick up the phone he thought of Dad saying what he didn't want to hear – that he wasn't going to come to his birthday party. So he kept putting off the call.

Eventually his dad solved the problem by phoning first, and once Harry heard his voice he couldn't stop the story tumbling out, in every detail. He missed out the part about Eddie teaching him to dance, and didn't really mention how scared he had felt; but anyway, the most important part was the puppies.

Dad was suitably
impressed. "So what
are they?" he asked.

"Maltipoos."

"That's a daft name.
Er … what about moodles?"

Harry laughed. "And that's not daft?"

"You could say you've got oodles of
moodles!"

Harry snorted.

"Hey, guess what I'm doing on this pad by
the phone?" Dad went on. "I'm doodling a
moodle!"

The silliest jokes make you laugh the
most. It was a minute or two before Harry
could speak again. He took a deep breath
and asked, "Are you going to come and see
these puppies, Dad?"

There was a silence on the other end.

Then Harry heard a voice in the
background, as if Dad's girlfriend had only

just come into the room. He heard Kim ask what they were talking about, and his father broke off to tell her all about the puppies. Harry heard her shriek with excitement and call out, "Give me that phone! I want to hear all about it from Harry." Her voice was warm and Harry was surprised at how much he wanted to tell her the whole story.

"Oh, I can't *wait* to see them," she said when he'd finished.

"Well," he began, wondering if he dared, "there's always my birthday party."

"What birthday party?"

"Didn't Dad tell you? You're both invited, because … y'know … Mum's friend Eddie'll be here, and…"

There was only the slightest pause before she added, "And Bonnie and the puppies too! Tell you what, Harry, I'm going to talk to that dad of yours and we'll call you right back."

Ten minutes later the phone rang. Heart thumping, Harry grabbed the phone – and there was Kim again. "Hello, love, I'm putting your dad on now."

"Harry? I've decided we'll come down for your party after all. Kim's desperate to see those puppies – as well as you, of course. All right, big guy?"

At that moment, Harry felt as if he was being watched. He turned. Sure enough, two  bright black eyes were staring at him from the box in the cosiest corner of their kitchen. Bonnie looked triumphant.

It was all systems go for his birthday party. Mr and Mrs Wilson took charge of the arrangements, but Harry's mum said she would help with the food and Eddie promised to be a waiter. Zack and Zena made guest lists. Everybody had a job.

Except Harry. He spent so much time with Bonnie and her puppies, the days whizzed by without him noticing. He was fascinated by the little creatures. He watched as they grew bigger and stronger; and then one day the first puppy's eyes opened. This one was a little boy – the one with identical black ears. The next day the second puppy could see. It was another boy, but with one black ear and the other white with a little daub of black, as if somebody had been careless with a paintbrush. Last of all, the white puppy who looked most like her mummy found herself blinking straight at Harry.

"Hello, little Snowdrop," he said without thinking.

So one puppy was named, but they couldn't think of names for the other two.

"Maybe we should let their new owners name them," said Mum.

Harry gasped. "But aren't we keeping them all, Mum? We can't give Bonnie's children away!"

"We can't live here with four dogs, even if they're small ones. We'll make sure all three go to lovely homes."

Harry frowned. He'd see about that!

His birthday fell on a Saturday, which was perfect for the party. As a special treat Mum brought him breakfast in bed (a bacon sandwich with loads of ketchup),

but the best present came a short while later.
She staggered into the room carrying the
cardboard box with Bonnie and her puppies
inside. Then, very gently, she lifted Bonnie
onto Harry's bed, where the puppies could
still see her.

"She wants to watch you open your
presents."

"Hello, Rabbit, I've missed you,"
whispered Harry, stroking her silky ears.

Mum gave Harry a cool new jacket he'd seen in a shop window. Eddie's present was a remote-controlled football-playing robot, and Eddie's sister had sent him a T-shirt with – of course – a motorbike on the front. Last of all Harry unwrapped a Viking archaeology kit from Bonnie and her puppies.

"Because she likes digging in the garden so much," Mum explained.

The rest of the day passed in a flurry of party preparations. Harry did nothing except play with his robot and stroke Bonnie – until Mum came and picked up the box again. "Rosie and I have decided they're all coming to the party," she announced. "They can stay snug and quiet in the little airing cupboard by their kitchen."

Harry was so excited he thought his heart would burst out of his chest. The plan was that everyone would gather first at the Wilsons' and he'd go round as soon as Zack called him. When his phone rang he ran.

The sitting room seemed full. Dad was standing in the middle with Mum at his side, and he put his arm round her when everybody shouted "HAPPY BIRTHDAY, HARRY!" And then they all clapped and cheered as Dad stepped forward to give him a hug.

The whole dance club was there, as well as some other friends from school, plus Susie and Princess Daisy, Eddie's sister and Bruce, Mum's friend Olga, the Wilsons' friends who'd gone on the picnic with them ages ago, and even Alan the smiling postman and his wife. Eddie came forward to give Harry's dad a glass of beer, and they nodded at each other.

"Where's Kim?" Harry asked.

"Where do you think? With those moodles!" said Dad.

And everybody laughed, Eddie loudest of all.

The next minute, Bruce started to chase Princess Daisy around the room, and Susie ran after him shouting, "You leave her alone, you bad dog!" – and the whole room roared.

It was a great party. There was music, some dancing, and they even played a few silly games that got everybody laughing. Naturally, there was a mountain of magnificent food as well as a pile of presents. Dad gave Harry an iPod shuffle and Kim gave him some walkie-talkie goggles. From Olga came an art set, and the dance club gave him two Latin dance CDs.

"Oh good, we can practise," said Zena, tucking her arm in his, and he went red.

The Wilsons gave him a rucksack. "For the next time we go camping!" said Zack with a grin. Harry felt very lucky.

But his best present was seeing Mum and Dad in the same room, with their new partners, all getting on just fine as the party went along.

But *something* was up. Zena and Kim kept whispering together, and disappearing to visit the puppies. At last they marched, hand in hand, to where Harry was standing with his mum.

"We've got something to ask you," Kim began. "You know Bonnie's got *three* puppies…"

"…and you don't want to keep them?" finished Zena.

Harry's Mum nodded.

"Well, I'd love to give one a home," said Kim.

"And so would I," said Zena.

Harry laughed to see his father start to protest, then stop. And Mr and Mrs Wilson did the same. After all, what was there to protest about, when the two of them wanted it so badly – and everybody could see that this was a brilliant plan?

Even Harry.

"So, Mum, does that mean we can keep Snowdrop?" he asked.

She smiled. "Yes, love, we can."

"Will you cope, Dad?" Harry asked.

He gave a comical shrug. "Oh, I guess we'll just moodle along."

Harry's mum nudged him with a grin. "And feed it on noodles, eh, Dave?"

Suddenly Harry wanted to laugh and cry all at once. He slipped away to the airing cupboard where Bonnie lay on her side, her three tiny puppies snuffling around her.

"Thank you, Bright Dog Bonnie," he whispered. "You know what you've done, don't you? You and your puppies – you've made us all related. Now we're one great big family!"

BONNIE looked up. There was Bruce, staring into the box as if he was proud of his puppies. She gave a little growl to make him keep his distance. She could tell that poodle was going to be a useless dad!

It didn't matter. Nothing mattered except the warm scent of her three puppies with their tiny mewling sounds and small paws pushing at her tummy to make the milk come.

And the taste of the chicken Mum chopped up each day, to keep her strong. And Harry's hand stroking her head, his voice all soft, telling her how happy he was.

Yes, Bonnie understood everything.
Bright dogs always know.

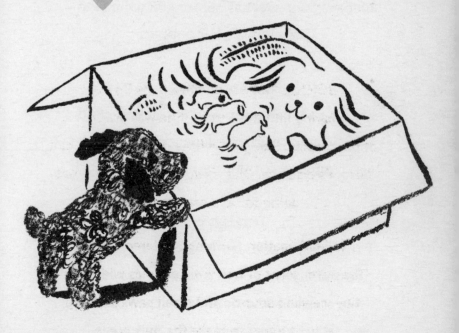

Puppy Timeline

Cute, cuddly ... and growing fast! Find out
how puppies develop week by week.

Pregnancy

A dog will be pregnant for an average of
63 days (nine weeks) before giving birth to
("whelping") her puppies.

New born puppy

For over a week puppies are deaf and blind.
They are completely dependent on their
mother for warmth and food.

Ten days old

Puppies' eyes and ear canals open between
ten and fourteen days after they are born.
They still prefer to be close to their mother
and their brothers and sisters (the "litter").

Three weeks old

Puppies start to get more active. The mother also begins to "wean" her puppies, gradually allowing them to suckle less and less.

Four weeks old

Puppies can begin to eat solid food.

Twelve weeks old

Between twelve and sixteen weeks old, puppies grow rapidly, including getting their adult teeth (lots of chewing!). Now they feel confident enough to leave their mother and puppy training can begin!

Bonnie
the Maltese

Bonnie is a Maltese dog. Maltese are sometimes called "toy dogs" because of their small size. They make perfect companions and family pets, because they are lively, playful and love human company. They're highly intelligent too.

In addition to their intelligence and affectionate personalities, Maltese dogs' good looks also make them popular pets! They are typically between seventeen and thirty centimetres tall, have brown eyes, black button noses, and long, silky coats that require lots of grooming. In fact, some owners prefer to keep their dog's coat cut short (like in the picture of Bonnie below). Maltese dogs are always white ... at least after a bath!

Historians think that Maltese dogs originally came from the Mediterranean, possibly the island of Malta. Both the Ancient Romans and Greeks wrote about  this small, white, friendly dog, so we can work out that Maltese dogs have been around for up to 2500 years.

Maltese: a small dog with a LOT of history!

Bonnie's Photo Gallery

Bonnie unveils her
perfect portrait!

Bonnie and Bel snuggle up
in the snow!

Bonnie wonders who's
behind the lens!

Bonnie is dog chic in the latest trends ...

... and toasty warm in her favourite jumper!

Bonnie's bag is packed — with small, fluffy dog!

Bonnie's Best Bits

**Have you read all six Bonnie stories?
Use this quiz to test your knowledge!**

(Answers on page 93)

Big Dog Bonnie

What is Harry's imaginary dog called?

What animal does Harry imagine Bonnie is like?

Best Dog Bonnie

What is the name of the grooming salon?

**What is the prize that Bonnie wins at the
dog show?**

Bad Dog Bonnie

What are the names of Zack and Zena's chickens?

What breed is Susie's dog Princess Daisy?

Brave Dog Bonnie

Who rescues Bonnie when she gets lost in London?

What job does Dad's girlfriend Kim do?

Continues overleaf.

Bonnie's Best Bits

Continued.

Busy Dog Bonnie

What is Zack and Zena's dad called?

What helpful thing does Bonnie do
on the farm?

Bright Dog Bonnie

What is the name of Mum's new
boyfriend?

What breed are Bonnie's puppies?

Answers: 1. Prince; 2. An Arctic fox (or "snow fox"); 3. Millionhairs; 4. A "Best in Show" rosette; 5. Egg and Chips; 6. A Chihuahua; 7. Dan (and his friends Baz, Pete and Smiffy); 8. She designs wallpaper; 9. Simon Wilson; 10. She stops the sheep from escaping through the open gate; 11. Eddie; 12. Maltipoo (half Maltese, half poodle!).

Love Bonnie? Then why not read all six of her tail-wagging adventures!

To find out more about the books and the real-life Bonnie who inspired them, visit belmooney.co.uk

Bel Mooney is a well-known journalist
and author of many books for adults and
children, including the hugely popular Kitty series.
She lives in Bath with her husband and real-life
Maltese dog, Bonnie, who is the inspiration
for this series. Bel says of the real Bonnie:
"She makes me laugh and transforms my life
with her intelligence, courage and affection.
And I just know she's going to pick out a really
good card for my birthday."

Find out more about Bel at belmooney.co.uk

Sarah McMenemy is a highly respected artist
who illustrates for magazines and newspapers
and has worked on diverse commissions all
over the world, including art for the London
Underground, CD covers and stationery. She
illustrated the bestselling City Skylines series and
is the creator of the picture books *Waggle*
and *Jack's New Boat*. She lives in London.

Find out more about Sarah at
sarahmcmenemy.com